Madeleine L'Engle

THE OT

HER DOG

Illustrated by
Christine Davenier

BOOKS OF WONDER
SEASTAR BOOKS
NEW YORK

SeaStar Books
A division of North-South Books Inc.

First published in the United States by SeaStar Books,
a division of North-South Books, Inc., New York.
Published simultaneously in Canada, Australia, and New Zealand
by North-South Books, an imprint of Nord-Süd Verlag AG, Gossau Zürich, Switzerland.

Library of Congress Cataloging-in-Publication Data is available.
ISBN 1-58717-040-x (trade binding)
1 3 5 7 9 TB 10 8 6 4 2
ISBN 1-58717-041-8 (library binding)
1 3 5 7 9 LB 10 8 6 4 2

Printed by Proost NV in Belgium

Books of Wonder is a registered trademark of Ozma, Inc.

For more information about our books, and the authors and artists who create them,
visit our web site: www.northsouth.com

For my great-grandsons,
Konstantinos John Voiklis and Cooper Hindemith Roy,
who bring light to all the dark corners
—Madeleine L'Engle

For my daughter, Josephine
—Christine Davenier

First of all,

I think you should know that
I am the one who **wrote** this book.
After all (contrary to opinion),
the author of a book is very important.
Please believe me: without the author,
a book would **never get written**.
So, I—Touché L'Engle-Franklin—

my mistress went away for **several days.**
And when she came back, she brought with her

another dog.

If you ask me, this was a great waste of money.
Dogs are expensive to feed and clothe,
and one dog is enough for any family.
I fail to see why I did not satisfy **all** requirements.

I have beauty, wit, and charm.

I have been on the stage.

I am very talented.

And until this other dog
was brought into our home
(without warning),
my master and mistress
seemed perfectly happy with me.

I am **very** **good** about sitting on **laps**.
In fact, I **love** sitting on laps.
I know of no other dog
who could sit on a lap for as **long** as
or with as much **patience** as I can.

So why another dog?

I **dance**, oh-so-daintily,

when it is time to **eat**.

My master and mistress
love to look at me.

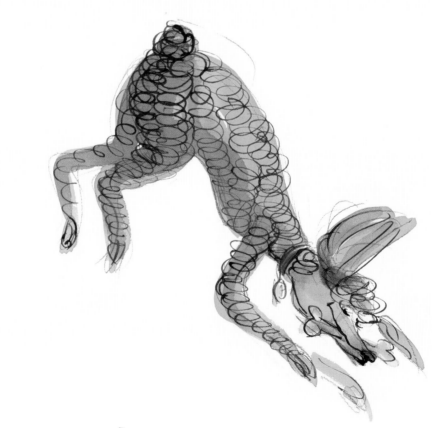

So why another dog?

I afford my master endless pleasure in his off-hours
when he bathes and clips me.
I can wear my ears long or short.
I sit still for hours while he snips off hair here and there.
No other dog would be so good and patient.

I am tremendously **useful** in such household tasks
as bringing home the groceries.
And I **always** tell my master and mistress
when the telephone or the doorbell rings.
No one could be

more efficient,

more energetic,

more conscientious,

or **louder**

about this than I am.

So why another dog?

But what's done is done.
The dog was brought home, and I had to learn
to make the best of it.

Nevertheless, from the start I noticed
a great many mysterious and **horrifying things**.
For instance,
when I am taken out to get some fresh air
I always have to **walk**—even when it **rains**.
The Jo is taken out in a carriage,
and when it rains
she doesn't have to go out at **all**.

And **another** thing.

My master and mistress keep putting on

and taking off white pieces of cloth around Jo's bottom,

called, for some obscure reason, diapers.

At first I did not understand the significance of this.

But when I did, I was deeply shocked.

When I have anything of that sort to do,

I go out into the street.

White cloths or no, I would **never** do it in the house.

At least one thing remained clear.

Of the two dogs, I was the most **important**.

You see, each night we would start out in our separate beds,
this dog called Jo, and I.

(Now, her bed may be a little more **fancy** and **froufrou**,
but mine is more **practical**.)

In the morning she would still be in her bed,
but I would not be in my bed.
Well, if that doesn't show you who's who around here,
I don't know what would.

And another thing.
This Jo-dog gets fed **several** times a day.
I only get fed **once**.
Of course, there may be a **reason** for this.

You see, I have frequently been told
that my tail is like a little chrysanthemum.
Jo-thing hasn't any tail at all.
Of course I am aware that, because of the dictates of fashion,
some dogs have their tails clipped.
But there is always something left.
And Jo has no tail.
Perhaps they think that if they feed her
and feed her,
she may grow a beautiful chrysanthemummy tail like mine.

And, by the way, our Jo—as well as having no tail—
has practically no hair.
Certainly not enough to brush.
So, when people come to call,
we have to put clothes on her.
All I need is a good hairbrushing.

If summer comes, can fall be far behind?
So said **the poet**.
Came autumn, and Jo-girl and I are almost the **same size**.
She has a little more hair but not much.
I am afraid she is just of an inferior breed called "baby,"
and there is nothing that can be done about it.

When the Jo-dog grew bigger
and bigger every day, and more and more **rambunctious,**
my master and mistress got a doghouse for her—
something I have been well-behaved enough **never** to need.
And now, when company comes,
I have to stay at the doghouse
and watch over our Jo.

I guess I have become more use there
than as the life of the party.
Ho hum . . .
It may be useful, but it's not nearly as much **fun.**
But since we have Jo-dog,
someone has to take care of her,
and I will do my part.

I must admit, though, that in our few conversations she's been most interested in everything I've had to say—

which is, I think, a definitely encouraging sign of
intelligence.

Therefore, I must admit that
in spite of myself . . .
in spite of the Jo-girl . . .
in spite of everything . . .
I am getting very fond of our other dog.
So, somehow or other, I have come to the
unpredictable,
surprising,
amazing,
astonishing,
astounding conclusion:

in every home there should be
at least
two dogs!

So now good-bye—and lots of love.
Touché

AUTHOR'S NOTE

Touché, a little grey poodle, came into my life when she was bought—for an exorbitant sum, I thought— during the rehearsals for Eva Le Gallienne's production of Chekhov's *The Cherry Orchard*. Of course, all the actors with dogs had wanted their pets in the show, but these other dogs were either intimidated by being in the theatre or, if they passed that first test, were undone by the noise of the party scene. So in came Touché, a born actress who wasn't in the least intimidated by the laughter and song of the party scene; she was quickly hired. Someone had to take care of her before and after the show, and I (the general understudy, who did everything that wasn't specified in the script) was lucky enough to get the job.

By the time the show was over, Touché and I had definitely "bonded," and there was no taking her away from me. By that time, Touché was thoroughly addicted to the adulation she received on stage. "Oh, that marvelous little dog! How did you teach her? She trains so easily! Can't you give her a little more to do? The audience adores her in that scene when she jumps up and tries to comfort—"

At this point Eva Le Gallienne would protest, a little wistfully, "That's supposed to be my scene." I could understand Le Gallienne's point of view.

There were a few less easily solved problems. For instance, travel. I lived in Greenwich Village. The theatre was in midtown. There was no way I could afford, on my Equity minimum salary, to take Touché back and forth in a taxi. So what to do?

I thought it over, and then I slung her over my shoulders like a feather boa, and she obediently hung there until we got to the stage door alley. Wherever I went, Touché went with me.

When Hugh Franklin was cast as Petya Trofimov, the young student who is Chekhov's mouthpiece, I expected the usual jealous annoyance from Touché. Not at all. Touché gave Hugh an appraising look, an interested sniff, and decided that he was all right. To my surprise, she let him brush her. She chose him to be her groom.

She did not come to our tiny little wedding, but otherwise she was with us night and day. And every evening, at the close of the play, she had her own special curtain call. We had to cut her down to one curtain call only, because she danced around and waved her paws at the audience and tended to take over the show, and the other actors complained.

When we had our first baby, I sat on the sofa nursing her, and Touché sat beside me, nursing a pink rubber hippopotamus. When she had her first litter, she was less concerned about the puppies than she was about her hippopotamus. She did her duty, but she wasn't really interested. But Touché and the puppies were so charming together that I took colored pencils and began sketching them. And that was the beginning of this book.

Her first love remained her true love: the theatre. There are not a great many roles written for a small grey poodle, but she did play Flush, Elizabeth Barrett's spaniel, in *The Barretts of Wimpole Street*. There's no way Touché looked like a spaniel; we just counted on her acting ability. The show had a long run, and Touché was happy. After it closed, everybody wanted to take Touché home—but she was mine, there was no questioning that.

There were no more plays at that time with dogs